Soda Pop
BEFORE THE STORE

BY RACHEL LYNETTE • ILLUSTRATED BY DAN McGEEHAN

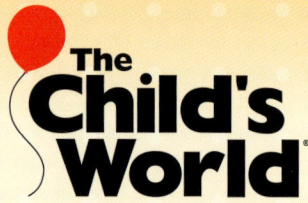

Published by The Child's World®
1980 Lookout Drive • Mankato, MN 56003-1705
800-599-READ • www.childsworld.com

ACKNOWLEDGMENTS
The Child's World®: Mary Berendes, Publishing Director
The Design Lab: Design and production
Red Line Editorial: Editorial direction
Content Consultant: Kyle W. Stiegert, Professor and Director of Food System Research Group, University of Wisconsin-Madison

Copyright © 2012 by The Child's World®
All rights reserved. No part of this book may be reproduced or utilized in any form or by any means without written permission from the publisher.

ISBN 9781609736828
LCCN 2011940078

PHOTO CREDITS
Dreamstime, cover, 1; Piotr Malczyk/Dreamstime, cover (inset), 1 (inset); Tudorache Aurelian/Bigstock, 5; Tischenko Irina/Shutterstock Images, 7, 30 (top left); Fotolia, 11, 30 (bottom left); Elena Schweitzer/Shutterstock Images, 13; Shutterstock Images, 15; Maria Toutoudaki/iStockphoto, 20; Mike Flippo/Shutterstock Images, 27; Avia Huisman Photography/Dreamstime, 29, 31 (bottom right)

Design elements: Dreamstime

Printed in the United States of America

ABOUT THE AUTHOR

Rachel Lynette has written more than 100 books for children as well as many teacher resources. She also writes blogs for teachers. Rachel lives near Seattle, Washington. She has a daughter in high school and a son in college.

Contents

CHAPTER 1	**All Kinds of Soda Pop**	4
CHAPTER 2	**At the Soda Pop Factory**	6
CHAPTER 3	**Soda Pop Syrup**	9
CHAPTER 4	**Fizz It!**	16
CHAPTER 5	**Into Bottles and Cans**	19
CHAPTER 6	**Labels and Packing**	24
CHAPTER 7	**Into Your Cup**	28

Soda Pop Map, 30
Glossary, 32
Books and Web Sites, 32
Index, 32

CHAPTER ONE

All Kinds of Soda Pop

There are all kinds of soda pop! Root beer, cola, and ginger ale are just a few. How many can you name? Soda pop is sold all over the world. It comes in bottles and cans. It also comes from a soda fountain at a restaurant or store.

What makes soda pop different from other drinks? Unlike juice or milk, soda pop is **carbonated**. That means it is full of tiny bubbles. Soda pop is almost always sweet and contains some kind of flavoring.

ALL KINDS OF SODA POP

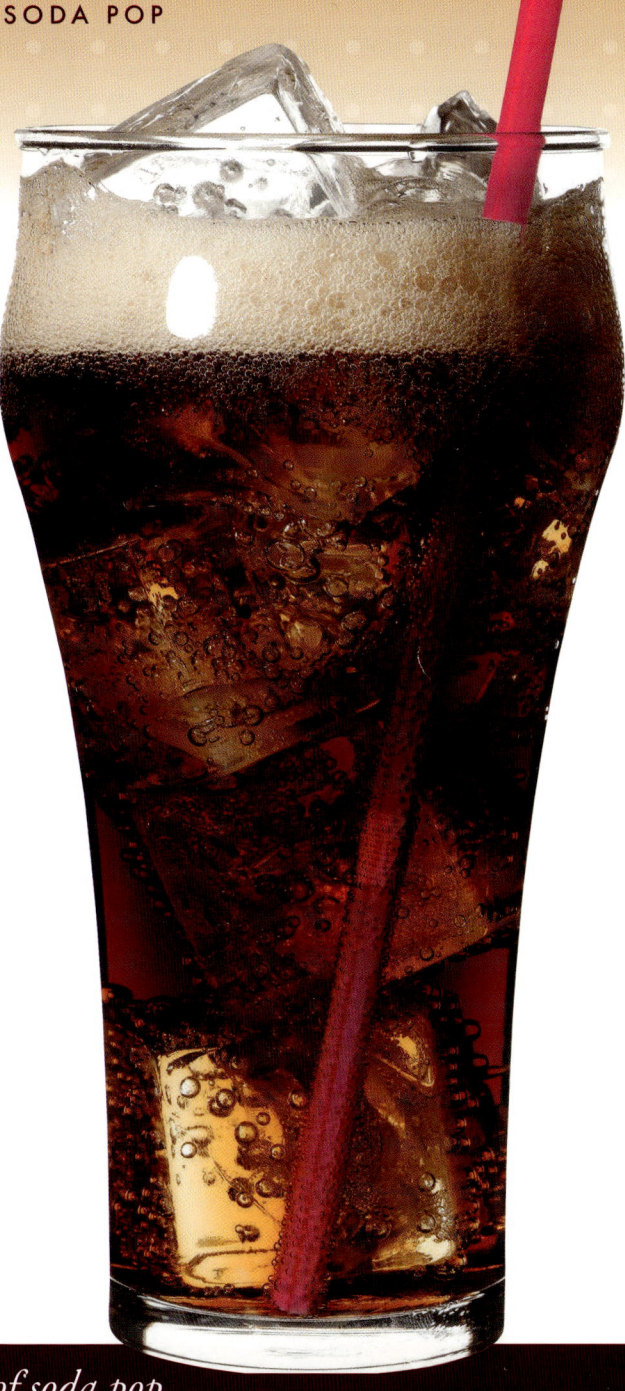

Have you thought about how soda pop is made? There are many steps. The first starts with water. Soda pop is mostly made from water. And that water needs to be very clean.

Cola is one kind of soda pop.

CHAPTER TWO

At the Soda Pop Factory

The water in soda pop is much cleaner than the water that comes out of your faucet. If the water is not clean, soda will not taste right or have the right color. The water is cleaned in stages.

First tiny bits of plants, animal matter, or minerals are taken out of the water. A certain gel is added to the water. The gel acts like a kind of glue. The tiny bits stick to it. They form a large glob called floc.

Most diet sodas are about 99 percent water.

Clean water makes soda pop taste and look good.

AT THE SODA POP FACTORY

Floc is caught as the water goes through sand and gravel filters. Filters allow liquid to pass through. Solids stick to the filters.

Next all **bacteria** is taken out of the water. Most bacteria is harmless, but some kinds can make you sick. The water is poured into a large tank. Some **chlorine** is added. It takes about two hours for the chlorine to kill the bacteria. Then the water is run through another filter. It takes out all of the chlorine. Now the water is ready to be made into soda pop!

CHAPTER THREE

Soda Pop Syrup

What makes soda pop taste so good? That sweet taste comes from the syrup. Each kind of soda pop uses a different syrup recipe. Soda pop syrup recipes are top-secret! Only a few people who work at a soda pop company know the secret recipes.

If you look at a can of soda pop, one of the first **ingredients** is sugar. Sometimes sugar has other

> There are about nine teaspoons of sugar in a 12 ounce (355 ml) can of cola.

SODA POP SYRUP

names. Glucose, high fructose corn syrup, and sucrose are all names for different kinds of sugars. The syrup in soda pop is made mostly from sugar. The sugar comes from sugar beets, corn, or sugar cane. For diet drinks, an artificial sweetener is used. These include aspartame and saccharin. They do not make people gain weight, unlike regular sugar.

The sugar used in soda pop comes to the factory as a liquid. It ships by tanker truck or train. This liquid sugar is mixed with other ingredients in a vat at the factory. These ingredients give soda pop

The syrup in soda pop is made mostly from sugar.

SODA POP SYRUP

its flavor and color. Some are natural, such as kola nut **extract** for cola-flavored soda and ginger for ginger ale. Small amounts of natural spices and oils from different plants are used in soda pop. Citric acid is also added to many kinds of soda pop. Citric acid comes from fruit. It gives the soda a slightly tart taste. Many kinds of soda pop contain **artificial** flavorings. They are made from **chemicals**. These flavorings are less expensive than natural flavors. The artificial flavors also make the soda smell good. This makes people want to drink the soda pop even more!

Caffeine is also in many kinds of soda pop. Caffeine gives people a little extra energy and makes the soda taste better. Other ingredients make soda pop look cloudy instead of clear or make it foamy. That is why root beer and ginger ale foam more than most kinds of soda pop. **Preservatives** keep the soda pop from going bad over time.

Citric acid comes from fruit.

SODA POP SYRUP

The syrup ingredients are mixed at the dosing station. Once the syrup is mixed, it must be cleaned to remove bacteria. **Ultraviolet** light kills the bacteria. It is shone into the tank that holds the syrup. The

Syrup is made at the dosing station.

SODA POP SYRUP

light destroys some of the chemicals the bacteria need to live. Another way to kill the bacteria is to heat and cool the syrup quickly. This is called **pasteurization**. Syrups that contain fruit, such as those for lemon-lime or orange soda pop, must be pasteurized.

Orange soda is pasteurized.

CHAPTER FOUR

Fizz It!

Now it is time to add syrup to the water. A machine lets out the right amount into the water. The water and syrup are blended together in a special tank. Have you ever tasted soda pop that is flat? It has lost all of its fizz. That is what the soda pop would taste like at this point. The soda pop is all done. It just needs the bubbles!

The bubbles in soda pop come from a gas called **carbon dioxide**. Carbon dioxide has no taste, color, or smell. A machine adds carbon dioxide to the soda pop.

FIZZ IT!

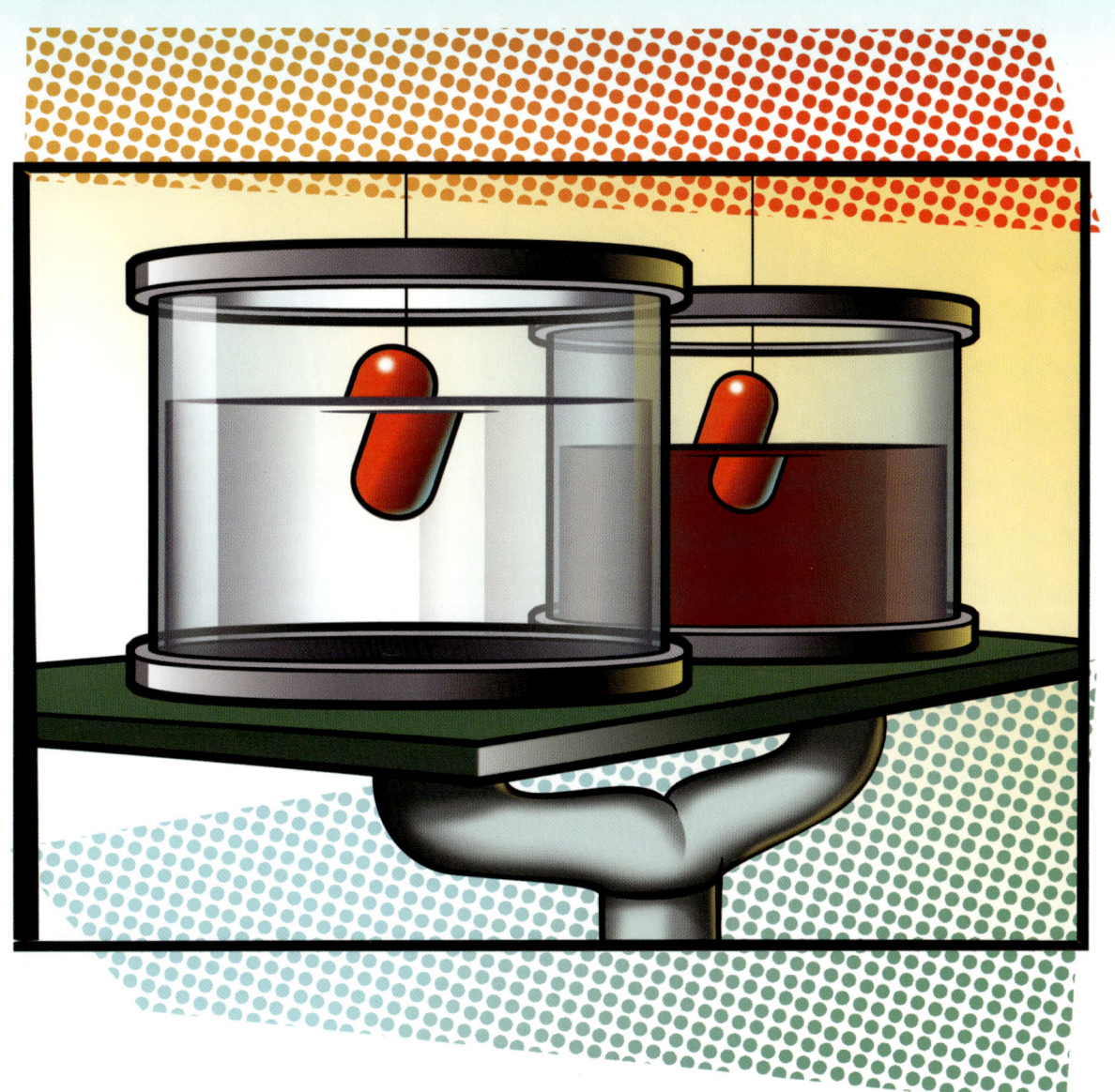

Syrup is added to the clean water.

17

FIZZ IT!

This is done in a large tank called a carbonator. The amount of carbon dioxide that is added depends on the kind of soda pop in the tank. Fruit-flavored soda pop has less carbon dioxide than other kinds of soda pop. Colas have more.

Carbon dioxide is added in the carbonator.

CHAPTER FIVE

Into Bottles and Cans

Now it is time for the soda pop to be put into bottles or cans. Most soda pop is sold in plastic bottles rather than glass. Some bottles have a single serving. The larger 2 liter (a little more than .5 gallon) bottles are enough for several people. Most cans only have one serving.

The bottles or cans come from a different

> Some bottling plants use recycled glass bottles instead of plastic.

All bottles must be washed before they can be filled with soda pop.

INTO BOTTLES AND CANS

factory. All bottles must be washed, even ones that are brand new. They need to be very clean before they are loaded into the filling machine.

Bottles travel to the filling machine on a **conveyor belt**. The filling machine carries the bottles around in a circle. The machine sucks all the air out of each bottle. Then a spout is put into the top and the bottle is filled

Machines fill the bottles with soda pop.

INTO BOTTLES AND CANS

with soda pop. The bottle is full after it has gone the whole way around the circle. The spout comes out and the bottle goes to the capping machine. The process is similar for filling cans.

The bottles travel in a circle around the capping machine. The machine screws a plastic lid tightly onto the top of each bottle. Glass bottles may have metal lids rather than plastic ones. The metal lids are crimped on the sides to keep them on the bottles. For cans, a machine attaches the pull-tab cover.

INTO BOTTLES AND CANS

Caps are screwed onto the bottles.

CHAPTER SIX

Labels and Packing

The plastic bottles still need their labels. The bottles and the soda pop cool as they move through the factory. If a label is stuck onto a cold bottle, the label could be ruined. It would get wet and not stick. **Water vapor** is in the air. It collects as tiny water drops on cold objects. To make labels stick, the bottles are warmed. They are sprayed with warm water and then dried with warm air. It is a bit like a carwash for bottles!

Labels are stuck onto the bottles.

LABELS AND PACKING

A machine puts glue on the backs of the labels. Then it sticks the labels to the bottles. Both sides of the bottle are brushed by the machine. This smoothes the label down on the sides to make sure it will not peel off. Cans and glass bottles do not need labels. Information is printed right on the cans and bottles.

Soda cans, small plastic bottles, and glass bottles are put into different kinds of packages. They come in four-packs, six-packs, ten-packs, and larger packs. Large plastic bottles are sold alone. Each different soda package is packed into larger boxes. Now they are ready to ship.

Cans of soda pop are sold in packs and cases.

People drink more soda pop in the United States than in any other country. Drinking too much soda is bad for you, though. It can cause people to gain too much weight. This can lead to many health problems.

CHAPTER SEVEN

Into Your Cup

The bottles and cans travel by truck and by train to stores where you can buy them! Some go to supermarkets or other stores. Other bottles and cans end up in **vending** machines. Not all soda pop comes from a can or a bottle. Soda pop also comes from a soda fountain. The soda fountain machines blend soda pop syrup with water and carbon dioxide. You just push a button and soda pop comes out of the spout and goes into your cup!

What flavor of soda pop do you like best? Soda pop can be fun to drink at a picnic or a party. Have you ever mixed two or three flavors together? If you add vanilla ice cream to root beer, you can make a root beer float. Yum! Enjoy some soda pop for a special treat!

Stores carry dozens of types of soda pop.

SODA POP MAP

1. CLEAN WATER
2. MAKE SYRUP
3. MIX SYRUP AND WATER AND ADD FIZZ

GLOSSARY

bacteria (bak-TIHR-ee-uh): Bacteria are small living things that are harmful or helpful. Chlorine kills bacteria in water.

caffeine (KAF-een): Caffeine is a chemical that is used in some kinds of soda pop and gives a person energy. Some soda pop has caffeine.

carbon dioxide (KAR-buhn dye-OK-side): Carbon dioxide is a type of gas that has no smell or taste. Carbon dioxide makes soda pop fizzy.

carbonated (KAR-buhn-ate-id): A carbonated drink has carbon dioxide in it. Soda pop is a carbonated drink.

chemicals (KEM-uh-kuhlz): Chemicals are substances made using chemistry. Chemicals add flavor and color to soda pop.

chlorine (KLOR-een): Chlorine is a gas that is added to water to kill germs and keep water clean. Chlorine makes the water used for soda pop clean.

conveyor belt (kuhn-VAY-ur BELT): A conveyor belt is a moving belt that takes materials from one place to another in a factory. Soda pop bottles move on a conveyor belt in the factory.

extract (ek-STRACT): An extract is an ingredient with water taken out, which makes it very strong. Kola nut extract is a natural ingredient.

ingredients (in-GREE-dee-uhnts): Ingredients are things that are added to a mixture, like items in a recipe list. Many ingredients are in a soda pop syrup recipe.

pasteurization (PASS-chuh-rize-ashun): Pasteurization is when food is heated to a high temperature to kill harmful bacteria. Pastuerization is used for fruit syrups.

preservatives (pri-ZUR-vuh-tivz): Preservatives are chemicals added to foods and drinks to keep them from spoiling. Preservatives keep soda pop from going bad.

ultraviolet (uhl-truh-VYE-uh-lit): Ultraviolet light is light that cannot be seen with a person's eye. Bacteria is also killed with ultraviolet light.

vending (VEND-ing): A vending machine is a machine that you insert money into and food or drinks come out. Soda pop can be bought in a vending machine.

water vapor (WAW-tur VAY-pur): Water vapor is water in the air that cannot be seen. Water vapor can keep labels from sticking to bottles.

BOOKS

Bodden, Valerie. *The Story of Coca-Cola*. Mankato, MN: Creative Education, 2009.

Spangler, Steve. *Fizz Factor: 50 Amazing Experiments with Soda Pop*. Salt Lake City, UT: Be Amazing Toys, 2007.

Tomecek, Steve. *Soda Bottle Science*. New York: Scholastic, 2006.

INDEX

bacteria, 8, 14, 15
bottling, 19–23
caffeine, 13
carbonation, 4, 16, 18, 28
chlorine, 8
flavorings, 4, 12, 18
floc, 6, 8
ingredients, 9, 10, 12, 13, 14
labels, 24, 26
pasteurization, 15
preservatives, 13
soda fountain, 4, 28
sugar, 9, 10
syrup, 9, 10, 14, 15, 16, 28
water, 5, 6, 8, 16, 24, 28

Visit our Web site for links about soda pop production: childsworld.com/links

Note to Parents, Teachers, and Librarians: We routinely verify our Web links to make sure they are safe and active sites. So encourage your readers to check them out!